Don't Tell Me to Smile

Julia Barron

D1452814

CONTENTS

For anyone who ever doubts themselves. Don't. You've got this.

Mom– Miss you.

Chris & Kirstyn– You are my whole heart.

For all intents and purposes, this is a completely fictional story with no real characters in a small-town bar far, far away. This, in fact, is not true in any way, shape, or form. If you are reading this and you frequent such an establishment, please disregard all statements that might pertain to individuals such as yourself. This book is intended for entertainment purposes only.

CHANGE IS HARD

ON THE RADIO THIS MORNING, THEY WERE TALKING ABOUT SLANG WORDS BEING USED BY GEN Z. SHIT WAS LIT AND NOW IT'S FIRE. I'M SIMPIN ON MY HUSBAND AND HE LOVES MY CAKE.

MY DAUGHTER IS OFFICIALLY MORTIFIED.

I WAS ON THE CUSP OF ACTUAL ADULTHOOD FOR WHAT FELT LIKE A SPLIT SECOND. IT HAS ARRIVED. I AM FULL BLOWN ADULTING.

I AM A WIFE, A MOM, I WORK FULL TIME, AND I'M ALSO TRYING TO PURSUE MY DREAM.

I ALWAYS HAVE ERRANDS TO RUN. OUR HOUSE STAYS CLEAN FOR WHAT FEELS LIKE A BLIP IN THE TIME CONTINUUM. WE ARE UP TO OUR EARS IN LAUNDRY ALWAYS.

I'M GOOD AT ADULTING, BUT I DON'T ENJOY IT. WHO DOES?

I LOVE TO FEEL LIKE I AM MAKING A DIFFERENCE AND BEING HELPFUL TO THE ONES I LOVE. HOWEVER, I AM ONE PERSON.

I'VE ALWAYS HAD FREEDOM. I'VE ALWAYS HAD RESPONSIBILITIES. I'VE ALWAYS ASPIRED TO BE THE BETTER VERSION OF MYSELF. I DIDN'T LOSE THAT. I PUT IT IN THE TRUNK AND FORGOT IT WAS IN THERE.

THE COLOSSEUM IS MY LIVELIHOOD AND MY WORST NIGHTMARE. IT IS THE ONLY FORM OF A

SOCIAL LIFE I HAVE. IT IS THE PLACE I MET MY
HUSBAND AND ONE OF MY BEST FRIENDS. IT
WAS A PART TIME JOB TO HELP SAVE FOR
COLLEGE AT THE RIPE AGE OF TWENTY. IT
TAUGHT ME LIFE SKILLS THAT WERE NOT
OFFERED AT ANY UNIVERSITY.

OUR DAUGHTER HAS GROWN UP IN THERE. SHE
WANTS IT TO BE HER FIRST JOB IN A COUPLE OF
YEARS. WE HAVE MIXED FEELINGS ABOUT
THAT.

IT'S NICE TO FEEL LIKE I'M GOOD AT
SOMETHING. IT'S EMPOWERING AT TIMES.
FEELING NEEDED IS ALSO GRATIFYING. UNTIL
YOU DON'T LOVE WHAT YOU DO ANYMORE, AND
THEN IT BECOMES A BURDEN. THE THOUGHT
OF LEAVING BEHIND A COMFORT ZONE AND
COWORKERS AND BOSSES THAT HAVE BECOME
LIKE FAMILY IS PARALYZING.

I THINK I WILL FEEL LIBERATED WHEN IT'S
TIME. I'M READY, BUT I DON'T THINK THEY
ARE. THE ACCOUNTABILITY I FEEL WHEN I'M
NEEDED AND DON'T COMPLY IS UNREAL. HAVE
YOU EVER HAD A FRIEND THAT REACHED OUT
TO YOU IN A DESPERATE TIME OF NEED, AND
YOU WERE UNAVAILABLE TO BE THERE FOR
THEM WHEN YOU'RE THEIR PERSON? HOW DID
THAT MAKE YOU FEEL? THAT'S HOW I FEEL
RIGHT NOW.

If only it wasn't so mentally and physically taxing.

I just want to be free.

I miss my family. My husband works day shift. When I arrive for work, he is heading home. My daughter gets off the bus around then as well. By the end of my shift, they are both usually already asleep.

I feel compelled to branch out, but I feel trapped. Maybe I have trapped myself.

So, can I learn to love my job again? Can I just push down what is calling me? What I aspire to be?

My dream?

How will I help pay bills? The resentment grows and is blossoming into something repulsive.

I am mad at so many things, but mainly myself for allowing this to transpire. I see it. I recognize it. I complain about it. Yet, I continue to allow it to happen.

Why?

Because I make good money.

Fake it until you make it, right?

Money isn't everything.

CHAPTER ONE

Why?

I am emotionally attached to an establishment that I feel like I helped build. I have watched it transform from a hole in the wall BBQ joint to a booming business. I have grown as it has, and we have had each other's backs always. It is a constant in my life that I will always be grateful for. I may feel like it's puppet at times but only I have the power to cut those strings. I have poured my heart and soul into this place for so long.

From the day the bar opened their doors to the public, I have been there; since day one. The mother hen of managers, the boss of all bosses, has been there since the beginning as well. She goes out of her way and beyond to ensure everything is fair to everyone all the time.

She taught me everything I know about bartending and a little about life, love, and friendships as well. She has become one of the best friends I have ever had. She does it all; much more than me. All the things, all the time. She knew my husband before I did, whom I also met at the bar I call my second home.

I wasn't even old enough to bartend when I applied. I heard there was a new sports bar in town, so I stopped in to see if they were hiring.

It was a crisp Fall afternoon. I was wearing my favorite green sweater dress and my high heeled boots. There was a group of men building the bar. They hired me on the spot.

I waitressed for a long time. I started college, I finished college, and a whole lot of stuff in between. I began bartending here and there when needed. Years passed and now I help run that shit.

I live comfortably. I have considered changing jobs multiple times since I graduated from college.

I make more money bartending than I would in any other field of work around here (pertaining to my degree). There are other options available now, but I have become complacent.

I feel a sense of ownership, pride, and loyalty to a place that I have referred to as a dumpster fire. You call it that and see what happens. I'll punch you right in the kisser.

My mom always taught me to fight with everything I have. Especially if it's something that I believe in. Keep fighting.

People depend on me here; people that I care about. I don't want to let them down.

CHAPTER TWO

Inner Monologue

I hit the ground running when I walk in to work, almost literally sometimes. I even stretch before I start my shift some days. I'm getting old, ok? Don't judge me.

Allow me to set the stage for you. Keep in mind that the bar where I work is the biggest and most popular one in town. Instead of 5-10 bar chairs, we have 17-20.

I walk in. Full bar. Holy crap. *Let's go. We've got this.* Scan the bar customers as I clock in...they're Gucci. Get caught up on dishes. Put glasses in the glass chiller. God forbid someone has to drink out of a warm glass. They might flip their shit.

Some asshole is thirsty/ drink deprived. Homeboy that has his own bar chair needs a shot. *"Hey Jules, can I get (insert hand gesture here to signify a shot because using words is so hard). Just when you have a minute..."* Sure, dude. I'm on it. Anything else for anyone? Of course... plate for Titus, ranch for Cassia, shot of fireball for what's her face, cold glass for shithead, chandelier, extended car warranty, whatever.

Someone gets up. *Thank you, baby Jesus. Don't clean it and no one else will sit there for a minute so we can get caught up a little bit. Fuck it.*

The owner walks in and stares at the only dirty spot at my bar like he can smell it as soon as he enters the building. *Don't make eye contact. Fuck. He's pissed. Bet he goes to check the ice next. We're busy, ok? Shit.*

Tickets rolling in. I hear my husband's voice in the back of my head complaining about the ticket machine in the kitchen that he hears in his sleep sometimes (*ticket, ticket, ticket, ticket*). Sometimes we just want it to stop.

Ten Vegas Bombs. *Easy. Bam. There you go. You're welcome. I'm awesome.*

Next ticket- 2 Pina Coladas (Fun fact: We always wish the blender was broken), 1 Rum Punch, 1 Gigi, 1 Rainbow, 1 Razorback, 2 White Russians, 5 Lemon drops, 1 Irish Car Bomb, and 3 tall Bud lights.

Fuck my life.

As a matter of fact, fuck all of you.

The server who rang that ticket in is staring at me like I can pull all of that out of my ass in .5 seconds. I bet she wonders what is taking me so long. *Please come try to do my job, I think to her in my head.* I hear "Jules" coming from 5 different people at the bar behind me, beside me, wherever they are, all at different intervals but in a manner of maybe 2 minutes.

They see me, right? I am one person. So rude.

Through gritted teeth depending on who they are (not going to lie, I cannot control my face sometimes), I ask what they want and tell them I will get it to them shortly. You know, after I finish this hellishly long ticket this dumbass rang in that must hate me on some level or another.

Why on earth would I want to make all these different kinds of drinks as fast as I can?

Oh. Right. That's my job. Sorry. Deep breath. Take a beat. Ok, back to it.

Another server is standing by my computer staring at me. I ask what they want with my face. *Words are over-rated, indeed. Just ask homeboy.* A server needs a discount for their table's ticket. Other server needs change.

Another server needs to tell me about a Karen at table 17 that needs to speak to a manager. On top of the full bar of customers and the tickets that won't stop rolling in, there is a line of waitresses forming at my computer waiting for something or other that only I can give them. *Lovely.*

Breathe. They are not your enemy. It is not their fault that you have so many responsibilities. You are on the same side/same team.

My pager starts buzzing on the bar. My customer's food is ready.

Finish bar tickets. Prioritize. *I have to make it to the Karen before she causes a scene. Scan the bar top. Will these dickheads be ok for five minutes or however long this is going to take?*

Check the needy Nancy's so they don't get upset when their drink is almost empty, and they don't see me anywhere making them a fresh cocktail. Ok, they're good for a quick minute.

Go. Smile big. Kill the Karen with kindness. *"Hi, I'm Julia. What's going on over here? What can I help you with?"*

"Ummm, I'm not sure what is the deal with my wings, but they taste disgusting. I don't want anything else. I just wanted you to be made aware of the situation and that it is just not acceptable."

"Oh. I'm so sorry about that. Are you sure we can't get you anything else? It will, of course, be on the house..."

"No. I'm fine. Please just take them" she says with the most disgusted look on her face like someone hocked a lugie straight into her wing sauce and it was the most horrific thing she ever tasted in her life.

"Sure thing. No problem. I'll make sure these are taken off your check. I'm so sorry about that. Is there anything more that we can do for you?"

Cool. Easy fix. Take the wings off her bill. Go to the computer. The server's entry number is not on the list. Sweet. I'll have to do it later.

Back to my bar. Said server finds me and looks puzzled. Like I have the only answers they've been searching for their whole life.

Gosh, it's not that serious. I tell them to put the wings on a separate check and I'll take them off later.

It's not rocket science. I'm too busy for this shit right now. While I was dealing with your table, the entire bar somehow downed all their drinks at the same time and are acting like I took a hiatus and was gone for over an hour.

My pager goes off again. The kitchen is pissed. It's so hot in there that their skin could literally peel right off. Picture their flesh slowly disintegrating right off their bones into your food. *Mmmm, so appetizing.* I feel for them.

Fuck those customers. They need a break. They hate their jobs. Poor guys. Someone give them a shot. I never went and got my food for my customer. No one brought it out for me, either. Now it's cold and must be remade. *Fucking Karen. Fucking servers. Fucking kitchen. Ughhhhh.*

If you are a server and you need something from your bartender/manager, please, for the love of God help them help you. Do a load of dishes, cash someone out, or put some glasses in the coolers. I guarantee you will be the first one they help with a discount, food complaint, check out, or whatever it is that you may need.

Everyone leaves. I clean the entire bar: plates, silverware, cups, coasters, spills, ketchups, etc. All cleaned up and ready to go. I'm exhausted and it's still only the beginning of my shift.

My last customer gets up and leaves. The rest of the bar is so clean it's pretty much sparkling. Fifteen seconds passes. A new customer arrives. They proceed to sit in the only dirty spot at my entire bar. It never fails. I scramble to clean up the stuff that they sat down right in front of as I greet them and ask them what they'd like to drink. They respond, *"Can I get a rag?"* as they point to a spot in front of them on the bar.

What is the science behind this? Really? It's insane. Seriously. Why? I cannot and will not ever understand it. There are 15 empty bar chairs with your name on it. Why choose the one and only spot that is dirty to sit down on and then proceed to complain about it? Why?

People love to complain. It makes them feel superior.

CHAPTER THREE

Bets are Off

Being in the service industry is a gamble. One I would go all in on if I had to bet.

If you are questioning whether to enter this field of work, prepare yourself. It's not for the faint of heart.

Proceed with caution. You might get sucked in. Cash in your pocket every day is something that is easy to get used to. People often transition into other jobs only to come back to serving. Make that money, honey.

I get paid by the hour, but barely. My income is solely based at times on who walks through those doors.

There are a great deal of connections that can accrue from bartending. I have worked at the same bar in the same town for over twelve years. Any profession that one could think of that they might need at some point or other, I probably know a guy (or girl).

When our outlets went out at our house because of the wiring, I knew a guy that knew a guy. Dentists, doctors, lawyers, cops (you name it)- they all go out to eat or have a drink on occasion. It's a small town. Odds are, if they have been into The Colosseum multiple times, I know them on a first name basis at least. I can hook you up.

Perks that come with the territory.

One of our superpowers is that we can usually pick up what you're putting down fairly quickly. Suffice it to say, we can tell if you are going to be a jerk straight out the gate. This is one of those times that I'm grateful to work with a bestie.

Our facial expressions are transparent. Laughter is hard to keep at bay.

We have been doing this together for so long that we have our rhythm down pat.

Especially on busy nights where all hands are on deck. I lean on her, and she leans right back. If one of us is not on top of our game, the other picks up the slack. We define balance.

We've been told that it's beautiful to watch us back there together (behind the bar, which is just a big square). We spin and twirl around each other and top off each other's drinks as we make them. We pour three beers at a time and stop the handles for each other as we walk by to grab a liquor bottle. We just *work*.

DJ's are loud. Bands are louder. We can't hear each other. We can't hear ourselves think. We learned to improvise. We attempt to read each other's minds.

Working in a restaurant is a unique lifestyle. You work strange hours. You bond with the people you go through hell with. You find commonalities. You are in this together. That's what we all want, isn't it? Just to not be alone in this(whatever *this* may be for you)? We may not act like it at times, but we are a team.

Some paths are just meant to cross. I have made so many friends working in this industry. Some have opened doors that I didn't even know existed.

CHAPTER FOUR

Slaves

Simply put, bartenders are glorified babysitters.

The responsibilities are endless.

Not only am I responsible for the customers that sit at my bar, I am also in charge of the tickets the servers ring in for the rest of the restaurant.

I am serving food to my customers, making drinks for everyone in the restaurant, and overseeing customer complaints. I also distribute food and make sure the servers are doing their jobs.

I wash all the cups from the restaurant, make sure the food isn't taking too long, and call-in help for the kitchen staff if needed. All the TVs with 15 different remotes must remain on appropriate sports channels. The patio lights are to be turned on when it is about to get dark. The trash needs to be taken out before it overflows. The ice bins need to be filled to the brim. Blah, blah, blah.

That is only to name a few. I failed to mention the solo duties on our downtime and the inventory of beer and liquor.

Smile.

The stuff the manager keeps up with behind the scenes in addition to her job as a bartender; let me tell you, it is insane. How one person is expected to do all of that is beyond me. She should be given a medal. She is a badass.

She deals with bullshit from all angles- customers, staff, upper management, and distributors of all kinds. She makes the schedule and works around everyone's other jobs. Not to mention requests off, call ins, drink specials, etc. She makes sure everything is clean all the time and that we're fully staffed. She makes sections for the weekends, deals with printing projects and band assignments and the list could go on and on.

Eat, sleep, and worship The Colosseum. Why?

Is this any way to live? We dedicate most of our time and pour all our energy into a business that at the end of the day doesn't belong to us. We get told thanks on occasion and that should be enough, right? To continue breaking our backs in the fast lane for as long as we can so that we can reap the benefits.

It's worth it, right?

We do all of that and are expected to have a smile on our face the entire time. It is also wise to have on makeup and look presentable. There is no privacy in a job like this, especially in a small town. You will be asked what's wrong and why you look so tired. You will also be asked if you slept last night, and why you did or didn't sleep.

Someone may also inquire what kind of milk you use in your cereal or what kind of moisturizer you use. It might all come from the same mouth that is twitching from thirst because it's been 2 minutes and 30 seconds since they finished their drink.

CHAPTER FIVE

Dumpster Fire

The ambiance of The Colosseum varies from day to night, by the day of the week, and sometimes by season. Any holiday that the owner deems worthy of transforming the restaurant, he will.

The Colosseum will morph into a fun house for children and adults alike. Halloween is his jam. He really goes all out. Have you ever been in a hurry and gotten your hair, apron, pen, (anything really) stuck in a fake spider web? He has them strewn over every spare inch of the wall. They look cool, but it's annoying. I'll leave it at that.

It is *the place* in town. It is the place to eat, the place to chill, and the place where everyone feels welcome. The energy is always good no matter who is there. There are songs on the jukebox. There are TV's everywhere, so you won't miss a minute of the game. You will always be greeted with a smile.

It is almost always busy, especially during football season. There are rarely open seats at the bar.

It is not a corporation. There is not anywhere else in the world exactly like it. It's unique and special. It's my home away from home.

You can sit by yourself and read a book if you want. You can spark up a conversation with a stranger at the bar. You can join the patio and the people that huddle out there.

You can people watch.

Sometimes, there are grown men singing loudly off key and taking selfies at the bar. They look like they're living their best lives. Admire or judge them. Your call.

Drunk people are funny sometimes.

It is an atmosphere that is unforgettable.

It's incredible in retrospect. It sounds relaxing and peaceful.

If only I could flip the coin, so you could see my side of it at times.

It's excruciating.

It's dreadful.

It resembles a dumpster fire.

CHAPTER SIX

Smile

What other job besides mine are you expected to have a smile on your face the entire time you're there?

When I am not speaking to a customer and am simply just doing what I am paid to do, I am not required to smile for the entire duration of my shift. I do not put Vaseline on my teeth to keep my smile plastered on my face. I may have to look presentable, but this is not a beauty pageant.

Say you are working on a big project. You're on a deadline. Your boss is breathing down your neck. The pressure is real.

You're so focused that there's no telling what facial expression your face has chosen to put on display (tongue sticking out, deep in thought, lost on I-40). You have people that are depending on you. In my case, they're only depending on me to refill their drinks, but just roll with it.

You get caught up and you're excited to finally exhale. You didn't realize that you weren't breathing properly because you were so focused.

Take a look around. Expect your eyes to be met with a bit of understanding from your customers. You have been working your ass off right in front of them this whole time. Their eyes do not express understanding. They just can't seem to fathom why you aren't still smiling.

The fuck?!? I'm supposed to smile at the cups as I wash them?

Apparently, I'm supposed to smile at the ice as I scoop it.

The liquor as I measure it.

The beer as I pour it.

Your dumbass face as I hand you your shit.

"It's not that bad."

"Smile."

"Your job is not that hard."

"Smile."

"Why aren't you smiling?"

Why aren't you smiling, Brutus? Who the fuck are you anyway? Why are you here?

Please come do my job and then tell me how hard it is.

Tell me to smile one more time.

I'll never smile at you again.

Eat a dick, Brutus.

CHAPTER SEVEN

I Know the Owner

Roll out the red carpet.

The sense of entitlement customers in a small-town bar carry is uncanny. Oh, you know the owner? *Cool. Me too.*

This does not, under any circumstance, make you special. Sorry.

I have two older gentlemen at my bar. One of them knows the owner.

Man #1 orders a tea. Man #2 orders a virgin martini.

If you don't know what is in a martini, this might seem like a normal drink order. Let me assure you, it is not.

A martini usually includes gin or vodka, maybe a little vermouth and some olive juice if it's dirty.

So, I ask the man if he means he just wants some olive juice.

He glares at me and then chuckles a little like I am the most retarded person on earth (so beneath him) and says he just wants a water.

How funny; refreshing, really.

What a delightful old man.

So, I put some ice in a cup and fill it with water.

Nope. Not what he wanted. He wanted a martini glass with water and an olive in it. Apparently *"in the real world"*, people order this way to look like they know what they're doing. *I should have known.*

Smile.

Caesar takes ten minutes to order a bud light after I list off all 14 of our drafts.

He stares at the taps for a while. He asks a few random questions about which IPA is more hoppy. I ask if he needs a minute to which he does not respond. He just continues to squint at the beers on tap.

If you need a minute, can you please just say so? I have other customers too.

There are bar regulars that have changed over time, ones that have stayed consistent, and some that have stopped coming in for a while and re-entered into the realm of drinks and décor that is The Colosseum.

The trends come in waves. There was a Packers crowd that came in for years with their cheese hats on and their team spirit on full blast. They were mostly an older crowd. They were so cheerful when their team was winning. It always brought a smile to my face.

The Blackhawks fan club that traveled in troupes loved to drink ten refills of coke and eat free popcorn. I always wondered if any of it even made it to their mouths because there was so much on the floor when they left. It's like their eyes were so glued to the game that they didn't even notice how much of a mess they were making. *Hockey is an intense sport.*

Chiefs fans are full tilt. They get drinks, dinner, and dessert. They don't hold back. They go big or go home. They are also loud. Most football fans are, though.

The crowd full of twenty somethings that order rounds of shots and want the jukebox at max amplification are a reoccurring theme.

Darts are like the super cool new thing now. People frequent our business night after night to play the same game. They sit at the same table and drink the same stuff.

They know the owner, too.

I wonder what trend will be next.

CHAPTER EIGHT

Worth It

The customers I save my smile for are pleasant, homeboy that has his own bar chair included. They smile. They seem to genuinely care if I am busy. They graciously wait a moment or two for me to get them their beverage.

They do not get angry. They do not wave their hands in the air at me when they need something.

They do not call or text the owner about a television not being on a sports channel. They know what they want when they sit down. They drink their drink. Sometimes they eat.

They do not interrupt me and my other customers. They are simply normal living, breathing human beings that chose to go out to eat or drink.

There are, of course, always exceptions to the rule. We have plenty of those. They are, at times, a pain in my ass. Other times, they are not a big deal.

We have regulars that have become a staple in our daily lives. They are familiar with the inner workings of The Colosseum.

They cook for us. They bring us candy. They go on coffee runs. They bring us homemade jam.

One of them cuts my fruit on day shift if I'm behind. One of them carries the ice buckets or cases of beer when he sees that I am struggling. They check on who is cooking and ask my husband to make them delicious food if he isn't behind because he's the best at it. They even tip him for it sometimes.

They are intuitive and experience my job with me, even though they are on the opposite side of the bar. It would not be the same without them. I so wish we could trade places at times.

These customers are worth it. Even when they annoy me (*insert hand gesture here*), they are a part of my life that I will always remember and miss about this job when I decide not to do it anymore.

There are people that come to this area for work every few months, or once a year, and it is always nice to see them too; like seeing an old friend. Some tip so well that I'd allow a hug if they really insisted. Just a hug, though. Don't get it twisted.

Our restaurant would not be the same without these types of people. The regulars are what keep us going. They keep the business running. They could go buy a case of beer for much cheaper and meet at one of their houses, but it wouldn't be the same. It's the aura that draws them in.

CHAPTER NINE

It Matters

I am frequently asked how long I've been at my job. I usually just respond with "*a long time*". When prompted, customers tell me they ask me this because it's obvious that I know what I'm doing. So, in other words, I'm good at my job. That is mainly true because I've been doing it for so long. I could do most of it with my eyes closed if I had to.

A big part of my job is being friendly and having a rapport with the customers.

Just a little while ago, I was taking an order from a customer, and he was simply asking me what I liked on the menu as he was perusing the food items. I was busy. My bar back arrived, and I sent her to retrieve his order because he was trying to have a conversation with me. I just wanted to make the drinks.

My head is usually held high. I used to be fearless. Life and loss have taught me differently. I prefer to keep my head down; do what is necessary and then retreat to my safe haven filled with my fur babies, my loves, and my favorite things.

I'm spent. I'm in search of something and it is not within those four walls anymore. I'm not sure it ever was.

My smile is gone; the real one anyway.

I do more than the bare minimum. I'm not hateful to my customers or co-workers. I keep smiling at strangers like I'm supposed to.

I am more negative than I would like to be at times. We all have our days. I'm trying, but it's taking a lot more energy than it should be.

I used to be such a private person, but this job has ruined me on so many things. When prompted continuously about what is bothering me on a bad day, I will probably let off steam. Like a teapot that's brewing. If you don't tend to it, it will boil over.

Keep poking and the bear will attack.

Plus, I'm a ginger. So, there's that.

Does it matter?

The answer is a resounding yes.

It matters if you smile.

It matters.

To the person dining alone to unwind, it matters.

To the person having a drink after a hard day, it matters.

To the couple having a date night, it matters.

To the group of friends catching up, it matters.

To the grump that looks like he just lost his dog, it matters.

Smiling may be the smallest act, the tiniest morsel.

It might be all the kindness you're able to portray, but it matters.

I promise, it matters.

Change is hard.

CHAPTER TEN

Service With a Smile

There are still days that I love my job. They are rare, but they still exist.

This usually happens when:

I'm working with a good crew that efficiently works together as a team. I don't have to worry about the floor (referring to the tables in the restaurant).

Customers are understanding and not douchebags.

Regulars come in that I am genuinely happy to see, thus I smile and actually mean it.

It's busy and the hours fly by.

The dishes and drink tickets don't pile up to where it seems impossible to get caught up.

I have *help*.

Someone brings me coffee.

The rush ends early so I have plenty of time to clean and stock. This means I will not have to stay until an ungodly hour to close the bar.

People are generous.

Customers drink leisurely and know their limit. If they have one too many, they arrange a ride for themselves.

Also, it's nice if they're happy.

Again, drunk people are funny sometimes.

It's relatively slow. I have been doing this for so long that the job itself is fairly easy.

It just comes natural to me at this point.

I don't hate what I do.

I generally enjoy people. I'm good with them.

I know how to keep them happy.

It just takes a toll after a while.

It is exhausting to fake being happy.

Just because I'm good at it, doesn't mean it is what I should be doing.

It is easier said than done, but like everyone else in the world, I strive to be personally fulfilled.

This job just isn't doing that for me anymore.

Someday, I will leave this place.

Until then, I will continue to greet you with a smile.

Tricks of The Trade/ Pearls of Wisdom

Say pardon my reach instead of excuse me.

Can I get you anything more? Not else.

Upsell.

Assume the man wants another beer if you can't get his attention.

Memorize everything.

Try to remember what they had yesterday, especially if you've never seen them before.

Separate tabs from the beginning.

Smile big as often as you can.

Kill people with kindness when they are rude. Some people just need to feel heard.

Treat every customer like they are your own.

Be a team player/ Go the extra mile.

Talk to customers as soon as they sit down anywhere. No one likes to feel ignored or unimportant.

Take a minute. Skip your turn for a table. It's ok. We've all been there.

If you are female, always address the woman at the table first. Don't even look at the male until you have addressed her.

Have fun. You are an actress. Put on a show if you want. Use an accent. Act happy as shit. Make them have an entertaining or at least pleasurable experience.

I promise, it's harder than it looks.

Proper Etiquette When Dining Out

Before I worked in a restaurant, I had no idea that these things were bothersome. Honestly, when I began bartending frequently is when I learned what not to do.

I used to ask my server/bartender so many questions. I was that girl. I never knew what I wanted to drink.

It's acceptable to do this. It is not frowned upon. Unless the person does not have time to answer your questions. In which case, they need an extra hand, but one is not always available. It is impossible at times to be as helpful as we "should" be to our customers.

Again, I am one person.

There's no handbook for being a good customer, is there? If there is, I'd like to read it.

Here's my take on it.

1. *Don't tell me to smile.*

Say it louder for the ones in the back. This is a whole mood.

There is nothing more annoying than being told to smile.

Haven't you ever heard that saying about telling a woman to calm down when she's mad?

Trying to bathe a cat? I don't remember the phrase. But you get my drift, right?

Servers and bartenders have lives just like everyone else.

Not only are we trying to prioritize the twenty things in our head so that we can stay on top of our shit, we're also probably worried about if our child has done their homework. Or, if our husband's migraine went away that he had earlier in the day. Or our dog's vet appointment for her fat tumor the following morning.

Whatever is going on inside our heads or at our home doesn't matter to you. I get it. We just serve you drinks. However, it matters to us.

We do not burden you with our problems. But, we are allowed to think about them while we wash dishes if we want to.

When we hand you your drink, we will reflexively smile. When we greet you, we will smile. When we ask you if you need anything *more*, we will probably smile.

Do you smile when you are worried about something? Or thinking about something unpleasant? Or checking off things in your head? Or making a mental note about something?

Cool. Neither do we.

2. *Don't move to a table without closing your tab at the bar.*

As previously mentioned, we survive basically off your tips alone. If you are waiting for people to join you, wait at a table with enough chairs for everyone.

This ensures that the appropriate server can get you a beverage.

Most people sit at the bar to wait because they don't want to be seen sitting alone at a big table.

I get it. However, you should put on your big boy pants and just do it. Sit there and wait. You'll be fine.

This is an issue because you are taking up a chair at my bar that I am not going to be compensated for. Unless, of course, you close your tab with me before you start a new one at your table when your party arrives.

Let's say a big tipper comes in and wants to sit at my bar. He or she cannot sit there because you are occupying said chair to wait for the rest of your party.

Said generous tipper has to find somewhere else to sit. Another server or bartender will now receive their tip.

You are unintentionally taking money right out of my pocket.

3.   *Don't make me feel inferior.*

Do not come in and act like you are better than us.

We run around a lot and get sweaty.

Our shirts are permanently stained from beer spills, ketchup, ranch, and bleach.

Leave your judgements at the door, please.

The fact that I have to wait on you if you sit at my bar does not make you better than me.

Your highness.

I do not live to serve you.

Well, I make a living serving you but that doesn't make you royalty.

Patron.

Play your part.

I am a real person.

Order your stuff. Eat/ drink it. Pay your tab.

Leave. No harm. No foul.

On to the next one. The cycle continues.

It does not have to be an arduous process.

4. *Don't touch me.*

Do not, under any circumstance, touch me or any other server or bartender. We do not endorse physical contact at the job site.

Common courtesy.

Human decency.

Even strippers have a hands-off policy. We are fully clothed and delivering food and drinks. Your $2 or $50 tip does not matter. It does not pay for hugs. Violating our personal space and getting inside of our bubble is not for sale.

Laughing at your dumb jokes, smiling when we don't want to, and having to wait on you for hours on end is seriously bad enough. Don't push it.

When we see you in any public place that is not our place of employment, do not try to hug us then either.

Do not make the situation awkward by trying. You can wave if you want, but that is it.

You are pathetic.

I hate you and I hate living in a small town just for this reason.

It is unfair and not cool.

Please don't touch me. Ever.

Also, don't touch each other.

Don't make out at the bar.

Get a room.

You are making everyone uncomfortable.

5. *Don't be a Karen.*

Do not get mad and complain about the wait time for your food when we are swamped.

Certain wait times are not acceptable, and we apologize and will try to make it up to you.

It is out of our control, and we would never make you wait that long on purpose.

However, when you can see the restaurant is full and we are running around like chickens with our heads cut off, please wait or leave.

Take your pick.

Being rude to your server and/or the manager really is unnecessary and will get you nowhere.

Do not order water with a side of lemons to make your own lemonade with our sugar packets once we drop it off. Lemonade is $2.45. Come on.

Do not order a coke and a water and never touch the water.

Do not ask me what you want and make me pick something for you to eat or drink and then order something else.

Don't pay as you go and then try to claim that the prices are different every time or argue about how many you've had.

Don't tell me you are ready to order when you are clearly not ready to order.

There is no rush. Take your time. I have plenty to do until you're ready.

Please don't make me stand in front of you for no reason while you read the entire menu.

Don't brush your hair at the bar. I applaud your personal hygiene, but people are trying to eat here.

If something gets sent back because they find a hair in their food, I will strangle you.

6. Don't ignore me.

Hello? Do I need to do a freaking jumping jack to get your attention?

How do you not see me standing here? Oh, they see me. I know they see me.

Please answer me.

Look at me at least and nod yes or no.

It just takes a second.

A courteous thumbs up would even be great.

Do you have any idea how rude it is to carry on with the conversation you're having?

I am trying to say hello. I am trying not to be inconsiderate.

Don't make me interrupt you. You are literally forcing me to be rude.

It is my job to greet you and get your drink order. You want me to do that, right?

Only at your convenience, I guess.

Fantastic.

Do not meet me with a blank stare or ask me to repeat myself more than twice. Clearly, I am asking you if you need anything. Drink refill? Any condiments for your sandwich? What else would I possibly be asking you? Use your brain, please.

You good? Cool. It's really that simple.

Don't ignore me only to need something as soon as I walk away from you. I have moved on to another customer. You had your turn. You can wait.

7. Don't order To-Go.

Or at least, don't make it complicated.

We do not have a To-Go person. When the phone rings, I must answer it.

In addition to taking your order, I must get your order ready by including the sauces that go with your meals. Close the boxes, check the ticket, bag them up, and so on.

I could have a full bar of customers. It doesn't matter. I still have to answer your call, address your questions, and take your order.

Don't argue with me about the menu items.

Don't place a huge order and expect me to put names on all of your boxes. I do not have time for that. If you must request this, please tip accordingly.

I do not expect a tip from a to-go order. It is not a requirement.

However, if I get behind with the customers that are tipping me because you were being complicated with your order? Please tip. It's just rude not to.

For the love of all things holy, do not tell me to hold on.

You called me.

I am busy.

This happens much more often than it should. It is the rudest thing ever.

Please do not do this.

8. *Don't be annoying about sports.*

I work in a Sports Bar. There are so many TVs.

Of course, we have the NFL package.

Do not argue about what game to put on the bar TV.

Yes, we will put that game on for you somewhere.

No, you cannot request a TV four hours prior to when the game starts.

You may come in to request a game on a certain TV and wait for it to come on.

First come, first serve. That's how it works.

That is how it has always worked.

That's how it should work.

Pretty simple stuff.

Nothing to phone home about.

9. Don't seek bar therapy.

Look, I know it's my job to talk to you, but I have shit to do.

I'll make you a drink, but then you've got to phone a friend or something if you need someone to vent to.

Do not try to strike up a conversation with me that is irrelevant when I have other customers to get to.

Small talk is fine.

I do not want to hear your entire life story, though.

In general, it's pretty obvious if you enjoy talking to someone.

Don't be oblivious to the fact that I am uninterested in what you are saying.

If I am busy, just don't talk to me unless you're ordering.

You could be the most intelligent person on the planet.

What you have to say could change my life or my perspective.

It does not matter in that moment.

Leave a note or something.

I do not have time to talk to you.

No connections are being made.

I am required to stand there while you speak.

You should be able to read the writing on the wall.

Take a hint.

Otherwise, I am considered rude.

I literally *have* to be nice to you.

It's the worst.

10. *Don't be complicated with your order.*

Drinks

Do not Google drinks that you had this one time at this one place.

We have a drink menu for a reason.

Even if we have the ingredients to make this special drink you want, it's super annoying.

Do not ask me to make your drink strong.

Order a double and you will be charged accordingly.

Don't order anything frozen. Whatever it is, we're out of that.

Do not ask me what's on tap.

I will automatically list all 14 of them. Then, you will probably just order a Bud Light.

Why make me waste my breath? Just curious? Fuck you.

Do not just say "I'll take a beer". Then, act annoyed when I ask: What kind of beer? Am I supposed to be psychic?

There are so many different types of beer.

Specify what you want.

Food

Read the menu.

Order off the menu.

Plain and simple.

We have what we have.

We serve what we serve.

Don't be ridiculous.

11. Do not get in our way.

Pay attention to your surroundings.

We are running our asses off and you are right in the line of fire.

Don't hover.

Please remain seated.

Do not wander around the restaurant and expect us to find you, either.

Sit the fuck back down and we'll get you a drink.

There is a narrow area between the server station, the bar, and the kitchen door.

Why do you think you can be over there?

Do you work here?

You are congregating in our space.

This is our bubble as a collective.

Get the h-e-double hockey sticks out of our freaking way, please.

We wish we could run you over.

Unfortunately, this is not allowed.

Move.

12. *Don't be a slob.*

If you are a messy eater, fine.

If you have messy children, also fine.

It happens.

It's our job.

Tip us extra to clean up your mess, though.

Please.

We have to take extra time to clean in between customers.

We do not have a janitor.

No one cleans up for us after we clock out for the day.

We do that ourselves; all of it.

We clean up the vomit in the bathrooms.

We unclog the toilets.

From the chairs you sit on to the floor where you walk, we clean that.

All of it.

13. *Do not come in just to watch the game.*

Must I reiterate that we make our living from tips that our customers give us?

There are TVs in a lot of establishments.

Must you pick ours to just pop a squat for hours on end?

Drink water and watch a football game. This is the life.

Oh, man.

Must be nice, pal.

Get a grip.

There are so many people that want to sit there and pay us for doing so.

If you are not ordering food or drinks, please go somewhere else.

Taking up a table all by yourself for hours is obnoxious.

We have a patio.

There are TVs out there.

Sit out there.

Or in your car.

I really don't care.

14. *Don't be a tough guy and try to pick a fight with someone.*

No one is impressed.

You look silly.

What are you even mad about?

Bro looked at you funny?

Doubt it.

Take a breath.

Let it go.

We provide an opportunity to unwind and get lit with your friends.

We do not promote bar fights.

On that note...

Please do not encourage violence.

Please help me diffuse the situation, not entice it to happen.

Arguments should not turn into brawls.

Drunk people shouldn't fight anyway.

You look dumb.

You are an adult.

Act like one.

We know you could take them.

No one is questioning you.

We believe everything you say.

Smile and nod.

No need to flex.

15. *Tip Accordingly.*

If someone is nice enough to pay your tab for you, please don't forget to tip.

Do not assume they tipped us for you.

They may not have tipped us at all.

You came in to eat or drink.

You expected to pay for something.

A tip is something.

It doesn't have to be extravagant.

Just something.

Please.

16. *Don't get angry when we ask for your ID.*

Consider it a compliment.

It is our job to ID you.

Why would you go to a bar without your ID?

This baffles me.

Be flattered, not offended.

"So & so served me the other day." No, they didn't.

Can I show you a picture of my ID? Sure, but I can't serve you unless you have the hard copy on you as well.

Will my cannabis card work? No.

I left it in my car.

I forgot my purse.

It's in my other coat pocket.

I don't care where it is, ma'am

If it is not presented to me, I cannot and will not serve you.

It's the law.

Bring your fucking ID.

17. Be respectful.

Don't hit on us.

We are there to make money.

If you must, don't be a creep about it.

Subtlety is existent.

It matters.

Choose your words wisely.

We can be flattered without feeling violated.

Aim for that.

Move stuff out of the way when we are trying to set down your food or drinks.

We only have two hands, and they are both full.

Use manners.

Don't shake the ice in your glass to signify that it's empty.

Don't interrupt me when I'm talking to other customers.

Don't snap your fingers at me or wave your hands in the air to get my attention.

I will get to you shortly.

18. Avoid controversial topics.

Please do not discuss religion.

Please do not discuss politics.

Please do not bring up abortion.

The pandemic.

Capital Punishment.

These are all fascinating topics.

Not at my bar.

This is not up for debate.

There is a time and a place.

This isn't it.

19. *Don't stay after closing.*

You have no idea how rude it is to hang out after we close.

You are interfering with our closing duties.

You are delaying our plans and/or our bedtime.

We cannot finish our work with you still sitting there.

We cannot leave until you do.

Is this the only job in the world like this?

Please don't make us hate you.

No, you cannot get another drink.

No, you cannot order food.

No, you cannot have change for the juke box.

No, you cannot ask for something else on the TV.

What you can do, is get the fuck out.

Please leave.

20. *Don't get wasted pants.*

When a customer downs drinks one after the other, my mind goes into overdrive.

Are they driving?

How much is too much? What is their tolerance level? Did they seem sober when they arrived? Should I offer them food again? Coffee? Water?

Great. So, it begins.

I will cut you off.

It is usually not pretty. Nine times out of ten, customers get so angry about it. What most of them do not understand is that it is a huge part of my job.

I can get in so much trouble and so can the restaurant for overserving.

It is a real thing. I have been cussed out, yelled at, and called every name in the book for doing so.

I don't care.

I would rather my customer thank me tomorrow or stay mad rather than them leave and something horrible happen.

Don't drink and drive.

It's so dumb on so many levels.

21. *Don't be extra.*

Extra anything.

Just *don't.*

Many thanks to everyone who made writing this book possible.

All my customers, past and present, thank you for inspiring me.

My older siblings, Ashley, Barton, and James, for supporting me in all my creative endeavors.

Ash, for always pushing me to reach my full potential.

Barton, for making me laugh and always knowing what to say. You just get me.

James, for keeping me grounded yet still encouraging me to fly.

Gina, thank you for being my person.

Toddy, my ride or die, this book would still be a very rough draft without your assistance. I wouldn't want to do life without you, boo.

Brigitte, thank you for believing in me. More importantly, thank you for helping me believe in myself.

DAD, FOR BEING AN EXTRA SET OF EYES WHEN I NEEDED THEM THE MOST.

CHRISTOPHER, FOR SETTING MY SOUL ON FIRE. YOU WILL ALWAYS BE MY MUSE.

KIRSTYN, MY MUNCHKIN, YOU ARE THE MOST ADORABLE CHILD ON THE PLANET. I AM A BETTER PERSON BECAUSE OF YOU. THIS BOOK IS BETTER BECAUSE OF YOU. THANK YOU.

VINCI, TESLA, DARWIN, AND PRUDENCE- MY FUR BABIES. THANKS FOR KEEPING ME COMPANY WHILE I NAVIGATED THIS ROLLER COASTER OF WRITING.

CPSIA information can be obtained
at www.ICGtesting.com
Printed in the USA
BVHW081639060122
625602BV00005B/119

9 781087 996875